Sister Aloysius Gets Ready for the First Day of School

by
Linda Etchison

Illustrated by Denise Plumlee-Tadlock

We greatly appreciate you taking the time to read this work. Please consider leaving a review wherever you bought the book and tell your friends and blog readers about the book to help us spread the word.

Thank you for your support.

ISBN: 978-1539652465

Printed in USA

Dedicated to my sister, Julia Winka,
who has unselfishly lent her time and expertise to the designing of
these books
and
to my dear friend and the illustrator of these books,
Denise Plumlee-Tadlock,
who has spent many hours to help make these books a reality.

May God bless you both abundantly!

The sun was just beginning to come up. Sister Aloysius peeked out the window of the little room that she shared with Sister Francis in the convent. It was so early that Sister Francis was still sleeping.

Sister Aloysius knelt down and offered her day to Jesus, then quietly dressed and tiptoed out of the room.

Sister was eager to get busy in her new classroom. In a few days, Sister Aloysius would be starting her very first year of teaching.

She was so excited, looking forward to the second grade class that had been assigned to her. Today she would be working in her classroom. What fun!

Sister quietly walked down the hallway of the convent so that she didn't disturb the other nuns.

She stepped out of the door of the convent into the courtyard between the convent and the church. It was still dark outside, but the wakening sun lit the way for her.

Instead of turning to go to the school, however, Sister Aloysius walked straight to the side door of Our Lady of Sorrows Church. She stepped into the dark, quiet church and made her way to the front pew. The tabernacle light shone red, sending a warm glow throughout the sanctuary.

Making the Sign of the Cross, Sister Aloysius genuflected and knelt down in the front of the church, bowing her head.

A feeling of peace and love filled her as she knelt in the quiet before Jesus in the Blessed Sacrament. Kneeling in the shadows of the dark church, looking at the tabernacle, she felt as if the arms of Jesus were around her.

As she gazed at the tabernacle, thinking of Jesus there in the Blessed Sacrament, she could almost see the face of Jesus looking lovingly at her, pleased that she had taken the time to come and see Him.

"I love You, Jesus!" Sister prayed silently. "Please help me to prepare for the school year in the way God wants me to. Please bless all the little children I will teach this year and all of their families. Help us all to grow in love for You this year. Amen." Sister finished the prayer in her heart.

Now she was ready to begin her work in the classroom. She got up, genuflected, and walked to the door of the church, blessing herself with holy water as she left.

She made her way across the courtyard to her classroom. "Jesus, I trust in You!" she whispered as she stopped for a minute in front of the Divine Mercy Shrine.

Sister Aloysius opened the door to the second grade room. "What a great room!" she thought. Through the low windows all along the opposite side, Sister could see the sun growing brighter outside. What a beautiful day it was going to be!

Sister looked around the room. Shelves full of books of all colors filled the spaces below the windows.

A big chalkboard covered the wall behind the large desk at the front of the room.

Bulletin boards covered the walls.

Sister walked over to the big desk. A pile of books and a list of names were already there. "Well, I had better get to work!" Sister Aloysius said to herself. "I have a busy day ahead of me!" She began making name tags for the desks and then placed the books on the desks for each child. Twenty desks filled the room.

Sister was so busy that she almost lost track of time. "Oh my!" she cried, "It's almost time for Mass!"

Sister hurried to the church joining the other nuns and parishioners for the early morning Mass.

After morning Mass and a light breakfast with the other nuns, Sister Aloysius hurried back to the classroom and happily continued getting ready for her first day of school.

She thought about the bulletin boards. "The children must have some colorful bulletin boards to greet them," she thought.

Sister Aloysius began planning.

Then she began cutting. She cut out letters. She cut out shapes. She cut out borders.

She drew pictures. She was so busy with her work that she even missed lunch!

Happily she began stapling the designs on the bulletin boards. She was deep in thought when all of a sudden, a voice brought her attention back, "Do you need some help, Sister?"

She looked around, but there was no one in the room. "Sister, I'm here at the window!" Sister Aloysius looked toward the open windows. There she saw two smiling faces looking at her.

"Well, hello, Pio! What a pleasant surprise! How nice to see you again!" said Sister.

"It's nice to see you too, Sister," said Pio.

"And who is this pretty little lady that you have with you today, Pio?" Sister asked as she smiled at the little girl with a nose full of freckles and two ponytails hanging over her ears.

"This is my sister Catherine," Pio said proudly. "She is in fourth grade."

"Well, hello, Catherine," Sister Aloysius said. "It's so nice to meet you. Pio told me he had a sister. I'm so glad he has brought you by to meet me!"

"Hi, Sister. I'm happy to meet you too. Pio told me about you and about Saint Aloysius," Catherine said happily.

"Sister, did you need any help?" Pio asked again.

"Well, yes, Pio. Help would be very nice. Run around to the door and come in," Sister Aloysius replied.

In just a few minutes, Pio and Catherine were in the classroom. "It's so nice of you two to help me," said Sister. "You can hand me the letters and pictures, and I will put them on the bulletin board. That will be a big help to me."

"Okay!" Pio and Catherine answered excitedly.

Sister, Pio, and Catherine worked hard getting all the bulletin boards decorated. Pio and Catherine chatted excitedly as they worked, happy to be doing such an important job helping Sister get ready for school.

"Oh, my!" Sister cried out suddenly. "Do you hear the chimes? It's 3:00!"

"Yes, Sister, it's 3:00," said Catherine.

"What's important about 3:00?" Pio asked.

"Well, Pio, 3:00 in the afternoon is a very special time. Can you think of a reason why it would be special?" Sister asked.

"I know," said Catherine. "Three o'clock in the afternoon is when Jesus died!"

"That's absolutely right, Catherine. Very good! And since 3:00 is when Jesus died, 3:00 is the Hour of Mercy!"

"Hour of Mercy? What does that mean, Sister?" Pio asked.

"Well, Pio, in the early 1900's, Jesus appeared to a nun by the name of Sister Faustina. He talked with her a lot about His Divine Mercy and about how we should ask for His mercy. He also told her we should show mercy to others. But another thing He told her was that 3:00 is the Hour of Mercy. He said that 3:00 in the afternoon is the special time of mercy and grace for the whole world," Sister explained.

"He told Sister Faustina that during this hour, if we pray, thinking of His Passion, He will refuse nothing to us that will be for our good."

"Pio and Catherine looked at Sister Aloysius with their eyes wide. "Really, Sister?" they said.

"Yes, really!" Sister replied. "It was during the 3:00 hour that Jesus' heart was pierced with a lance and blood and water flowed out for us all. When Jesus died on the cross for us, He gave every little bit of His blood for us. That is what makes 3:00 the Hour of Mercy," Sister Aloysius explained.

"Sister," Catherine said quietly, "that makes every day at 3:00 a very special time, doesn't it?"

"Yes, Catherine, and Jesus is very merciful to visit Sister Faustina and remind us all about His mercy and the 3:00 hour. That's why it is so good to stop wherever we are at 3:00 each day and thank Jesus for His mercy," Sister explained.

"Yes, Sister, and ask Him for the help we need," said Pio.

"And for help for our friends and family!" Catherine added.

"Yes, that's right!" said Sister. "And we can pray for people that we do not even know. We can pray for anyone who is sick or poor, or anyone who is unhappy or who does not know God. We can ask for God's mercy for these people too," Sister finished.

"Yeah! That way we can help other people too!" said Pio.

"That's right," said Sister. "Now I think I'll head to the church to pray for a few minutes. Would you both like to come with me?" Sister asked.

"Oh, yes!" Pio and Catherine replied.

"Well, let's go see Jesus then!" said Sister, and she headed to the church with the children skipping along beside her.

Dear Parents,

The following bits of information and references are included to offer you some resources in discussing items from the story with your child.

Visit to the Blessed Sacrament

Sister Aloysius gives us an example of devotion to the Blessed Sacrament when she stops in for an early morning visit to the Blessed Sacrament before she begins her day. In the story we notice the candle burning near the tabernacle, reminding us of God's presence abiding there night and day. Jesus loves for us to come and spend time with Him as He waits in the tabernacle.

Jesus is truly present – Body, Blood, Soul, and Divinity – in the tabernacles of our Catholic Churches and chapels. Through the words of consecration by the priest at each Holy Mass, the hosts and the wine become the Body and Blood of Jesus Christ. This transformation of the bread and wine into the Body and Blood of Christ is called *transubstantiation*. The appearances of the bread and wine remain the same, but the substance has changed.

Jesus gave us this tremendous gift of Himself at the Last Supper on Holy Thursday, the night before He died. The words of consecration used by priests at Mass today are the very same words used by Christ at the Last Supper when He instituted the sacrament of the Holy Eucharist. We have only to look at the words of Jesus Christ himself to know that what we receive at Mass is indeed the Body and Blood of Christ. *"Take and eat; this is my body...Then he took a cup; gave thanks, and gave it to them saying, "Drink from it, all of you, for this is my blood of the covenant which will be shed on behalf of many for the forgiveness of sins..."* (The New American Bible Matthew 26:26-28)

In His great love for us, Jesus has even bolstered our weak belief throughout time with many Eucharistic miracles such as that of Lanciano, Italy in the Eighth Century A.D. when a monk saying Mass had doubts about Jesus' real presence in the Eucharist. After the consecration, the host was visibly changed into Flesh and the wine into Blood. Scientific testing has proven that the Flesh and Blood is real human Flesh and Blood from human heart tissue with type AB blood. These Sacred Species, left in their natural state for twelve centuries still miraculously remain today for the faithful to venerate.

With this tremendous gift of Christ to us, it is no wonder that the Church encourages regular, worthy reception of the Holy Eucharist as well as adoration of the Eucharist outside of Mass as Jesus is reserved in our tabernacles.

Some things Jesus has said to His saints about the Eucharistic adoration...

- *"I have a burning thirst to be honored by men in the Blessed Sacrament, and I find hardly anyone who strives, according to My desire, to allay this thirst by making Me some return of love."* (Words of Jesus to St. Margaret Mary Alacoque)

- *"A Holy Hour of Prayer before the Blessed Sacrament is so important to Jesus that a multitude of souls go to Heaven who otherwise would have gone to hell."* (Jesus revelation to Blessed Dina Belanger)

- *"...beneath these rays (from the Eucharist) a heart will be warmed even if it were like a block of ice or hard as rock..."* (Jesus to Faustina, *Diary* 370)

Related Scripture Passages
    Body and Blood of Christ (1 Corinthians 11:26)
    Living Bread (John 6:48-54)
    Last Supper (Matthew 26:26-28; Mark 14:22-24; Luke 22:19-20; 1 Corinthians 11:23-24)

Catechism of the Catholic Church
    CCC 1333, 1337, 1339, 1341,1353, 1365, 1373-1376, 1382, 1392, 1394, 1402

Holy Water

As Sister Aloysius enters and exits the church, she blesses herself with holy water. By making the Sign of the Cross with holy water we as Catholics are professing our belief in the Trinity – God the Father, God the Son, and God the Holy Spirit. We are also recalling our baptism in the Trinity. In addition to the use of holy water in various rites of the Church, holy water is also used by the faithful in their homes.

Holy water is a sacramental of the Church. Sacramentals, such as holy water, are blessed by a priest. Various blessings exist for blessing holy water. Outside of Mass, the priest has the discretion to choose which blessing to use. Some blessings contain a minor exorcism such as in the following excerpts:

O water, creature of God, I exorcise you in the name of God the Father Almighty, and in the name of Jesus Christ His Son, our Lord, and in the power of the Holy Spirit. I exorcise you so that you may put to flight all the power of the enemy, and be able to root out and supplant that enemy with his apostate angels; through the power of our Lord Jesus Christ who will come to judge the living and the dead and the world by fire... May this, your creature, become an agent of divine grace in the service of your mysteries, to drive away evil spirits and dispel sickness, so that everything in the homes and other buildings of the faithful that is sprinkled with this water may be rid of all uncleanness and freed from every harm. Let no breath of infection, no disease-bearing air remain in these places. May the wiles of the lurking enemy prove to no avail. Let whatever might menace the safety and peace of those who live here be put to flight by the sprinkling of this water, so that the health obtained by calling upon your holy name may be made secure against all attacks. Through Christ Our Lord. Amen.

(Powerful Prayers That Make Things Happen: Prayers for Blessings, Breakthroughs, Healings, Miracles, Wonders & Exorcism by Rev. Fr. Mbaka Ejike C. pp.102-103 "69 Exorcism of the Water")

Or

I command you in the name of God the Father almighty, in the name of Jesus Christ his Son our Lord, and in the power of the Holy Spirit. Be water now no longer in the power of our enemy, but availing rather to put all his power to flight, to dislodge that enemy, with all his rebel angels, and to rid the earth of them; through the power of Jesus Christ our Lord who is coming to judge the living and the dead and the world by fire. Amen.

Let us pray.

O God,... May this your creature be your servant now in religious rites. May it have henceforth the power which divine grace can give it, to drive out demons and to ward off diseases; so that in the homes of the faithful and wherever the faithful may be, all that this water touches may be unsullied and wholesome. May no breath of contagion linger there, no taint of corruption. May the snares of the lurking enemy fall asunder. And if anything threatens the safety or the peace of those who dwell there, may it be banished by the sprinkling of this water. Thus may that wellbeing, which they sought when they called upon your holy name, be shielded from every assault. Through Christ our Lord. Amen.

(Manual of Minor Exorcisms: for the Use of Priests - compiled by Bishop Julian Porteous (Catholic Truth Society, Publishers to the Holy See p. 36-37)

Prayer

By this holy water and by Your Precious Blood, wash away all my sins O Lord.

Related Scripture Passage
    Numbers 5:17

Catechism of the Catholic Church
    CCC 1668-1673

The Hour of Mercy

Sister Aloysius did not want to miss going to the church to pray for souls during the three o'clock hour – the Hour of Mercy. In doing this, she is following our Lord's instructions to St. Faustina when He said, **"At three o'clock, implore My Mercy, especially for sinners; and, if only for a brief moment, immerse yourself in My Passion, particularly in My abandonment at the moment of agony. This is the hour of great mercy for the whole world. I will allow you to enter into My mortal sorrow. In this hour, I will refuse nothing to the soul that makes a request of Me in virtue of My Passion…"** (*Diary* 1320)

Jesus wants us to remember His death for us by venerating His death at 3:00 p.m. every day to obtain grace for the whole world. During the three o'clock hour, we honor and glorify God's mercy by remembering His Passion and Death and we obtain graces for ourselves and others.

If we are not able to visit Jesus in the Blessed Sacrament, like Sister Aloysius did, we can meditate for a moment on God's Mercy wherever we are and implore graces for ourselves and others.

Prayer given by Jesus to St. Faustina which, if said **"with a contrite heart"** will obtain for souls the grace of conversion:

"O Blood and Water, which gushed forth from the Heart of Jesus as a fount of Mercy for us, I trust in You." (*Diary* 187)

Related Scripture Passages
   Rich in Mercy (Ephesians 2:4-5)
   Delights in Mercy (Micah 7:18)
   God's Mercy (Psalm 25:6-7)
   God's forgiveness and forgiving others (Matthew 6:14; Romans 9:15-16)
   Merciful from of old (Deutronomy 4:31)
   God's mercy (Titus 3:4-6)

Catechism of the Catholic Church
   CCC 1829, 2447

Special Resource
   Diary of Saint Maria Faustina Kowalska: Divine Mercy in My Soul (Marian Press 1981)

Made in the USA
San Bernardino, CA
07 February 2018